BOYZ RULE!

Park Soccer

Felice Arena and Phil Kettle

illustrated by
Gus Gordon

First published 2003 by
MACMILLAN EDUCATION AUSTRALIA PTY LTD
627 Chapel Street, South Yarra, Australia 3141

This edition first published in the United States of America
in 2004 by MONDO Publishing.

For information contact:
MONDO Publishing
980 Avenue of the Americas
New York, NY 10018

Visit our web site at http://www.mondopub.com

04 05 06 07 08 09   9 8 7 6 5 4 3 2 1

ISBN 1-59336-366-4 (PB)

Library of Congress Cataloging-in-Publication Data

Arena, Felice, 1968-
    Park soccer / Felice Arena and Phil Kettle ; illustrated by Gus Gordon.
    p. cm. -- (Boyz rule!)
    Summary: Luis and Billy pretend to be soccer stars and have their own
    competition in the local park. Includes related soccer facts and questions to
    test the reader's comprehension.
    ISBN: 1-59336-366-4 (pbk.)
    [1. Soccer--Fiction.] I. Kettle, Phil, 1955- II. Gordon, Gus, ill. III. Title.

PZ7.A6825Par 2004
[E]--dc22

                                                                    2004047630

Project Management by Limelight Press Pty Ltd
Cover and text design by Lore Foye
Illustrations by Gus Gordon

Printed in Hong Kong

Contents

Billy   Luis

CHAPTER 1

Saturday Selection

Best friends during the week, Billy and Luis become weekend sports rivals. The park at the end of the street turns into a sports stadium. Saturday mornings can never come fast enough for these two champions.

Billy "You wanna play soccer?"

Luis "Yeah. Guess that's why you brought your soccer ball."

Billy "So, Hot Shot, what country do you wanna be?"

Luis "I think Italy. '*Forza Italia!*' How about you?"

Billy "I'll be Brazil—they won the World Cup."

Luis "Only because they didn't have to play Italy."

Billy "Yeah, really. Let's pick teams—I'm first. I want Beckham."

Luis "Beckham? He plays for England—you'll have to make an offer for him if you want him for Brazil."

Billy "He told me England can't play
anymore and he wants to play for
Brazil, as long as I'm captain. He
thinks I'm awesome."

Luis "Whoever told him that hasn't
seen you play."

Billy "We'll see, loser."

Billy and Luis pick their teams. Billy goes for Beckham because he thinks he'll want to switch from England to Brazil. The game is ready to begin!

CHAPTER 2

Start-up

The boys pretend to be sports commentators....

Luis *"There's excitement in the air here at the stadium. Both teams have just completed their warm-ups. The crowd is a little restless waiting for the great game ahead but it won't be long now...."*

Billy *"The grandstands (usually referred to as big trees) are filled with fans (commonly known as birds), all cheering for their favorite team. The goal posts (or trash cans to those in the know) have been lined up and the game is ready to go."*

Billy "Who kicks off?"

Luis "Me."

Billy "Why you?"

Luis "Because you asked and I want to."

"Italy has won the toss and they've decided to kick off first. Luis, the greatest player ever for Italy, hopes to take advantage of the lack of skill shown by Brazil in recent games."

Billy "*Brazil, captained by Billy the Brilliant, hopes that Italy might have eaten too much spaghetti before the game and will be slow to start. This could give Brazil the chance to kick some great early goals.*

Well, go ahead, Luis, kick the ball."

Luis *"Just waiting for Renaldo to get into place. Yes! Lucky Luis passes to Renaldo. He passes the ball back to Luis. Renaldo knows how good Luis is, moving like a champion. Then Luis slips past Billy."*

Billy *"Italy and their captain don't know how good Brazil's captain is. Billy tells Beckham to get the ball. Beckham stops to check his hair— it feels good so it must look good. Beckham lets Billy attack Lucky Luis. Billy runs through Renaldo— that's easy. He drops to the ground holding his leg. Billy keeps going, determined to get the ball from Luis."*

Luis "You've got no chance of getting the ball from me. You're too slow."

Billy "Me, too slow? I'm a lot faster than you are."

Luis "In your dreams."

Billy *"Renaldo gets to his feet. Billy runs at him again. Renaldo hits the ground. Billy's tackle is so fierce that he knocks all Renaldo's hair off, except for the little front part. Billy's eyes are on Luis, watching to see which way he turns."*

"Billy the Brilliant slides and knocks Luis's legs out from under him. Luis hits the ground. Now the trainer is running onto the field. He looks a lot like Luis's dog. He's licking Luis's face. This must be the latest technique in sports medicine to fix sore legs. Luis gets to his feet."

Luis "Do that again and I'll practice my Kung Fu on you."

Billy "We're playing soccer, not Kung Fu fighting. Maybe we can do that next week."

Luis "At least I get a penalty shot at the goal."

Billy "I never heard the ref's whistle blow."

Luis "Well, it did."

Luis takes a firm stand. He refuses to play anymore until he gets his penalty shot at the goal. The boys decide that they should take a break.

CHAPTER 3

Time to Rest

The boys walk away from the park.

Luis "So, what are we going to eat?"

Billy "Let's go to your place. Your
mom makes really good cookies.
I really liked those ones we had
last time."

Luis "Well, I liked what your mom gave us last time. I know what we should do."

Billy "Yeah? What?"

Luis "Let's have some at my place, then some more at your place."

Billy "Cool. You wanna swap shirts?"

Luis "Nah, mine's good luck. But I like yours. Where'd you get it?"

Billy "Renaldo gave it to me."

Luis "Like I really believe that!"

The boys go to Luis's place. They eat as much as they can, then they go to Billy's place. Billy's mom gives them some cookies, which they demolish in a few seconds. They head back to the park.

Billy "You wanna finish the game?"

Luis "I've got a penalty shot in front of the goal."

Billy "Let's just say the game is a tie."

Luis "We could make a different team. Maybe we could call the team the U.S. and we could both be the star players."

Billy "So who'd be captain?"

Luis "We should both be captains— that would make us the best team in the world."

Billy "How about we get Renaldo and Beckham to play for us? They'd love to play on a great team like ours."

Luis "Yeah, with two great captains like us!"

The new captains of Team U.S.A. walk back to their spot.

CHAPTER 4

The Shoot-out

The boys continue to call the game.

Luis *"After a long hard final in the World Cup soccer, which has lasted five minutes, the siren rings. Team U.S.A. and England are zero–zero."*

Billy "We have to have a shoot-out."

Luis "How many shots at goal do we get?"

Billy "As many as we like—it's our game. We make the rules."

Luis "Let's get four shots each. What about Renaldo and Beckham?"

Billy "They can sit out. They never did much in the game—we were the stars!"

Luis "Yeah, we were much better than them. They didn't even show up, and they still got paid tons of money."

Billy "All we get are cookies."

Luis "I'm going to go first because I didn't get to have my penalty shot when I was captain of Italy."

Luis and Billy take their penalty shots. Of course they get all their shots in. England has lost another final and the U.S., as usual, has proven that they are the best in the world. Billy and Luis celebrate their great win by running around the park and waving their shirts above their heads.

Billy "We won! We won! We're the champions of the world!"

Luis "We played so well. You were pretty good."

Billy "I know. So were you. We're an awesome team, probably the best in the world."

Luis "We're the coolest. I think our shirts really brought us good luck."

The boys start to walk home from the park, undefeated champions of the world.

CHAPTER 5

What's Next?

Billy and Luis think about their next big decision....

Luis "What should we do now?"

Billy "You still hungry?"

Luis "Yeah, a little. Let's go to your place for some more of your mom's cookies—I really like them."

Billy "Look at your dog. It won't stop peeing. It just peed on three trees in a row. It must have drunk the biggest bucket of water."

Luis "Dogs pee all the time."

Billy "So what should we do next weekend?"

Luis "Let's build something."

Billy "Yeah, maybe a new kennel for your dog. And Dad said he'd take me to watch soccer. Wanna come?"

Luis "Will Beckham and Renaldo be playing?"

Billy "I think they might be busy—
I'll ask them! I'm starved."
Luis "So, what's new?"

Billy

BOYZ RULE!

Park Soccer Lingo

Luis

goalkeeper *Not* the person who makes sure the goalposts are on the field before the game starts! The goalkeeper is the player who stands in the opposing team's goal area and tries to stop the other team from scoring a goal.

field The playing area you play on when you have a game of soccer.

goal When the ball is either headed or kicked into the goal area.

manager The boss of the coach of the soccer team. When you start to play serious soccer you have a team manager.

Park Soccer Musts

☞ You can have as many players as you want on each team.

☞ All players will also be referees.

☞ Goalposts can be trash cans, or even two jackets put on the ground.

☞ If the ball gets kicked into a tree, the person who kicked it has to get it.

☞ Take plenty of food to the park.

☞ Have as many food breaks as you like.

☞ Sometimes it is good to stop midway through a game and have a kicking contest. See who can kick the soccer ball the farthest.

☞ Referees don't need whistles in park soccer. They just have to yell really loud.

☞ You can wear any shirt you want when you're playing park soccer.

☞ Make sure you have a lot of fun— that's always the most important rule when you play park soccer.

Park Soccer Instant Info

 The longest time spent spinning a soccer ball on one finger is 4 minutes and 21 seconds.

 The farthest distance traveled while controlling a soccer ball is 26.2 miles (42.2 kilometers).

Brazil has won the most soccer World Cups. They have won five—in 1958, 1962, 1970, 1994, and 2002.

A professional soccer field measures around 110 yards long and 80 yards wide (100 meters by 73 meters).

 The size of a regulation soccer goal is 24 feet wide and 8 feet high (7.32 meters by 2.44 meters).

Soccer is called "football" in most countries besides the U.S.

A soccer match is played by two teams of 11 players each, with one player on each team acting as a goalkeeper.

The first professional soccer game was played in 1885.

Think Tank

1 What teams do Luis and Billy pretend to play on?

2 What do Luis and Billy use for goalposts?

3 How many players are on a soccer team?

4 What does a goalkeeper try to do?

5 What happens if you foul a player?

6 What is your favorite position to play in soccer? Why?

7 Is it important to warm up before playing soccer? Why?

8 Do you think it's okay to foul another player while playing soccer? Why or why not?

Answers

8 Answers will vary.

7 It is important to warm up so you don't pull a muscle during the game.

6 Answers will vary.

5 If you foul a player, the player gets a penalty kick and you get into trouble with the referee.

4 A goalkeeper tries to stop the ball going through the goalposts.

3 There are 11 players on a soccer team.

2 They use trash cans as goalposts.

1 Luis pretends to play on Italy's team, and Billy pretends to be on Brazil's team.

How did you score?

- If you got most of the answers correct, then you could be the captain of your soccer team.

- If you got more than half of the answers correct, then it's park soccer for you.

- If you got less than half of the answers correct, keep practicing!

Felice → ← Phil

Hi Guys!

We have lots of fun reading and want you to, too. We both believe that being a good reader is really important and so cool.

Try out our suggestions to help you have fun as you read.

At school, why don't you use "Park Soccer" as a play and you and your friends can be the actors. Set the scene for your play. Find some props and use your imagination to pretend that you are at your local park about to start your first World Cup soccer match.

So...have you decided who is going to be Billy and who is going to be Luis? Now, with your friends, read and act out our story in front of the class.

We have a lot of fun when we go to schools and read our stories. After we finish, the kids all clap really loudly. When you've finished your play your classmates will do the same. Just remember to look out the window—there might be a talent scout from a television station watching you!

Reading at home is really important and a lot of fun as well.

Take our books home and get someone in your family to read them with you. Maybe they can take on a part in the story.

Remember, reading is a whole lot of fun.

So, as the frog in the local pond would say, Read-it!

And remember, Boyz Rule!

BOYZ RULE!
When We Were Kids

Felice

Phil

Felice "Did you play soccer as a kid?"

Phil "Never, I only ever played football."

Felice "I think you would have made a great goalie."

Phil "Why's that?"

Felice "Because of your great defense in football now."

Phil "Thanks, man. I agree—I was a natural at most sports."

Felice "Don't go overboard. You're not at World Cup level yet."

Phil "What about park level?"

Felice "Definitely!"

BOYZ RULE!

What a Laugh!

Q How do you light up a soccer field?

A With a soccer match.